Can You Do This, Old Badger?

Written by
Eve Bunting

Illustrated by
LeUyen Pham

HARCOURT, INC.
San Diego   New York   London

Library of Congress Cataloging-in-Publication Data
Bunting, Eve, 1928–
Can you do this, Old Badger?/Eve Bunting;
illustrated by LeUyen Pham.
p.   cm.
Summary: Although Old Badger cannot do some things as easily
as he used to, he can still teach Little Badger the many things he
knows about finding good things to eat and staying
safe and happy.
[1. Badgers—Fiction. 2. Old age—Fiction.]
I. Pham, LeUyen, ill. II. Title.
PZ7.B91527Can   2000
[E]—dc21   98-39809
ISBN 0-15-201654-6

Printed in the United States of America

B D F H J K I G E C

The illustrations in this book were done in gouache on
Arches 200-pound rough press watercolor paper.
The display type was set in Elroy.
The text type was set in Galliard.
Color separations by Bright Arts Ltd., Hong Kong
Printed and bound by Phoenix Color Corp., Rockaway, New Jersey
This book was printed on totally chlorine-free Nymolla Matte Art paper.
Production supervision by Stanley Redfern and Ginger Boyer
Designed by Lori McThomas Buley

To our newest Little Badger,
John Desmond Bunting

—E. B.

With all my love,
to Jenn, to Marie and, especially,
to Shino

—L. P.

It was the time between sunset and dark. Old Badger and Little Badger walked along the forest path.

Little Badger jumped a little jump.
"Can you do this, Old Badger?"
  "I can but not very well," Old Badger said.
"I used to be a good jumper. But now my legs
are stiff."

Little Badger tucked himself into a ball and rolled down the slope of the path. "Can you do this, Old Badger?"

"Maybe I could still do it. But it would be hard for me. I used to roll very well." Old Badger picked leaves and twigs from Little Badger's fur.

Little Badger climbed up a bent skinny tree. "Can you do this, Old Badger?"

Two blackbirds danced out of the leaves into the sky.

"I can still climb. But only if I have to," Old Badger said. "And I would climb backwards because it's easier."

"That's good to know." Little Badger came down and took Old Badger's paw. "It's sad that you are old now and can't do many things."

"There are some things I can't do now," Old
Badger said. "But you help me remember how it
was when I was young. And that makes me happy.
Besides, there are lots of things I can still do.
And lots of things I can teach you." He pointed.
"See where the ground is muddy from today's rain?
There will be earthworms there. Come and eat."

Old Badger was right. There were wriggles and
wriggles of fat earthworms on the damp earth.
"Yum," said Little Badger.
They ate and ate.

When they were finished, Old Badger went
to the stump of a tree. He raked at it with his claws.
"This is how you get the mud out from between
your toes," he said.

"I can show you where to dig for bulbs of wildflowers in spring," Old Badger said. "In summer I can take you where the juiciest blackberries grow. I can teach you where the field mice make their nests. I can help you find honeybee hives. But remember, never go into a hive face first. You will get your nose stung. A wise badger does not go in where the bees come out."

"I wish there was a honeybee hive right here, right now," Little Badger said.

Old Badger sniffed the air. "There may be one in that rotting log."

There was.

They clawed through the top and got to the beehive before the bees got to them. Afterwards they walked along, licking the honey from their paws.

"Yum," Little Badger said.

They stopped by a wide stream.
"I can teach you to fish," Old Badger said.
"I didn't know badgers could fish!" Little Badger was surprised.
"Some can."

They stood in the stream.

Old Badger flipped a shining fish onto the bank.

Little Badger saw one swimming below. He tried to catch it, but it slithered through his paws. "It looks easy," he said. "But it's not."

"You'll learn," Old Badger said. "It takes time."

They sat on the bank of the stream to share
Old Badger's fish.

"How do you know so much?" Little Badger
asked, his mouth full of fish.

"Because I have been around for a long time.
And because, many years ago, an old badger taught
me. Someday you will be an old badger and you
will teach a little badger what you know. That's
the way it was planned." Old Badger wiped Little
Badger's mouth with the back of his paw.

"Will that little badger love me as much as I love you?" Little Badger asked.

"He will," Old Badger said. "That's part of the plan, too. And now it's nap time."

"Is that another part of the plan?" Little Badger asked.

"It's another part of *my* plan," Old Badger said.

They curled side by side in a hole on the bank of the stream. The night air was cool on their fur. Their paws were still sticky with honey and silvered with fish scales as together they slept, under a badger moon.